SOUL
MAKE A PATH
THROUGH
SHOUTING

Soul Make a Path Through Shouting

Cyrus Cassells

COPPER CANYON PRESS

Haiku by Bashō from *On Love and Barley* translated by Lucien Stryk
(Penguin Classics, 1985) copyright © Lucien Stryk, 1985. Reproduced by
permission of Penguin Books Ltd.

Excerpts from *An Interrupted Life* by Etty Hillesum, English translation
copyright © 1983 by Jonathan Cape Ltd. Reprinted by permission of
Pantheon Books, a division of Random House, Inc.

Excerpts from *Letters From Westerbork* by Etty Hillesum, English trans-
lation copyright © 1986 by Arnold J. Pomerans. Reprinted by permission
of Pantheon Books, a division of Random House, Inc.

Publication of this book is supported by a grant from the National
Endowment for the Arts and a grant from the Lannan Foundation.
Additional support to Copper Canyon Press has been provided by the
Andrew W. Mellon Foundation, the Lila Wallace–Reader's Digest Fund,
and the Washington State Arts Commission. Copper Canyon Press is in
residence with Centrum at Fort Worden State Park.

Library of Congress Cataloging-in-Publication Data

Cassells, Cyrus.
Soul make a path through shouting : poems / by Cyrus Cassells.
p. cm.
ISBN 1-55659-066-0 : cloth – ISBN 1-55659-065-2 : paper
1. Gay men – United States – Poetry.   2. Afro-American gays – Poetry.
3. Afro-Americans – Poetry.   I. Title.
PS3553.A7955S65   1994
811´.54 – DC20   94-9842

COPPER CANYON PRESS
P.O. BOX 271, PORT TOWNSEND, WASHINGTON 98368

SINCERE THANKS to the Rockefeller Foundation Center in Bellagio, Italy, the Massachusetts Artists Foundation, the Helene Wurlitzer Foundation, the Corporation of Yaddo, the Millay Colony, the Fine Arts Work Center in Provincetown, and to the National Endowment for the Arts.

My gratitude to Nancy Swisher for her kindness in allowing me to paraphrase two lines from her play, *Erase to Heaven*, and to Ian MacMillan for his novel, *Proud Monster*, which was one of the inspirations for "Fleur." "A Shadrach Chorus" was inspired by Susan Griffin's *A Chorus of Stones*, and alludes, imaginatively, to the lives of the painter Charlotte Solomon, and the music teacher Alfred Wolfsohn.

For their strong and ever-ready support, I would like to thank Martín Espada, H. Joan Freeman, Ken and Peggy McIntosh, Mark Nepo, my parents, and most of all, Terry Pitzner.

Grateful acknowledgment is made to the editors of the following journals, in which these poems first appeared (some in earlier versions): *The Boston Review, Callaloo, The Fine Arts Work Center Anthology* (Sheep Meadow Press), *The Indiana Review, The Kenyon Review, Muleteeth, Ploughshares*, and *Provincetown Arts*.

This book is dedicated to the memory
of Etty Hillesum
(1914–1943)

This book is also dedicated to Sulak Sivraksa,
peacemonger, truthteller, and soul-of-pearl,
who has been unjustly accused in Thailand.

Sulak, you have what the cudgel,
the scorner's curse, the fist
can never fathom –
freedom from hatred

CONTENTS

The day will come when, after harnessing the winds, the tides, and gravitation, we shall harness for God the energies of love. And on that day, for the second time in the history of the world, man will have discovered fire.

> *– Teilhard de Chardin*

Come, see real
flowers
of this painful world.

> *– Bashō*

SOUL
MAKE A PATH
THROUGH
SHOUTING

Down from the Houses of Magic

in Provincetown

I

Now the moon darns the moor with its fabric of
   minnows,
And the sea rushes with the ecstasy of ants.
Down from the houses of magic, a healing wind sweeps,
Down from the houses of magic.
On Gull Hill, in the flaming garden, God flings
A fistful of robin redbreasts – razzamatazz.
And the reed of the supple mind bends and shivers,
And the choirlike, match-stemmed, fiercely gallant
   flowers:
Johnny-jump-up, pert buttercup, anemone, peony,
   lupine,
The first lightning-white rose dying to open
Beneath the systole and diastole of a starry night,
Iris, allium, the proffered chalices of tulips,
The colors of a fabulous dusk in Tunisia;
Coming soon, a pleasure of freesias, a pleasure.
Such tintinnabulation – listen:
All the prayer-wheels of April-into-May luster
Spinning God-drunk – till finally beside
The moon-daft willow, slack as a marionette,
The frenzy of scotch broom,
The fleet-souled orioles marshal, at wolf's hour,
Then sally in one brilliant will.

Abundance begins here – at the sea lip:
On the Cape I've come to God and Proteus, come to rest in
　　wild places:
Whisker-still galaxies of marshlands,
Beaches where I pause and study
The Atlantic, teal and taciturn, the Atlantic, glittering and
　　fluent,
As on blond days fishermen stagger
And bluefish wake to the breathless dream of land.

Having combed eerie dunes,
I have been on desolate moons, wind-worked to pure
　　scrimshaw,
And found deer, cranberries, a plum dusk,
Pools of sweet water carved into sand.

The streets stink of fish, after the dark
Gimcrack shawls of squalls and rain.
I amble through rumors of shipwrecks, ghosts,
Sense the red broom-sweep of the beacon even in my
　　sleep –

I have my tremendous window.
The moon-jacklit boat comes to it, shimmering,
And the bride-sweet cirrus cloud,
And sometimes the streak of a squirrel, like the deft, sudden
Stroke of the watercolorist, whose brush distills the bay.

And now, clear and fugitive, in jack-in-the box brilliance,
The baby whale blooms:
Wild world, wild messenger – you are the moment's crown,
　　sea-loved:

When providence brims to the outermost land,
No lack, no lack, but in my human mind –

Midsummer.
And after belligerent sun, twilight brings
A muezzin of sea-wind,
And the soul of the garden bows,
A praise in the earth:
Among Turk-cap lilies, suddenly,
In the willow's cool hair,
The breath of God –

Now I stand in the garden
Like a messenger proclaiming
I am Cyrus, and I am here,
Amid Lilliputian canon-flowers –
I surrender! I surrender! –
Under starry dippers pouring
Into a vast and holy dark –

One day on Gull Hill I wept and prayed:
Let this earth become a heaven –

Beyond the garden, the wall of clematis:
The world with its rills of blood,
The blue and virulent cell where a man was flayed
To make a flag of human skin –

Tonight the moon makes a silver threshing-floor of
    the sea.
Beside the moth-claimed path, the stone seraph decays,
The stiffened body of a finch –

The rose is no paraclete.
A keen star plummets into the heart's cup, the summer
    grasses.

And the blue earth resumes its measureless dialogue
Between catastrophe and plenty.

The dirty, nail-bitten hand
Of a Black Lear,
With the green and pink
Bracelets of a woman,
Inching its way
Through garbage:

Even in the garden on Gull Hill,
I see that hand:
All day rocking back and forth
Between Turk-cap lilies and the trash –
Till at last words spill out,
Ones I shrink from:

Are you hungry all the time?

Yes, all the time –

O grant us strength to fashion a table
Where each of us has a name –

From autumn to autumn, teach us
How to breathe, endure,
In the shadow of the sickening weapon;

Teach us how to blossom,
If the sky is acid,
The garden marred –

We move through the world with its drastic reds,
Its discord,
Seeking balm in all things:
Mother's milk, the dream of reunion –

Not enough to hate suffering,
Hate war,
But to jettison at last
All duality, division,
To discern
God-in-the-guise-of-the-stranger,
God-in-the-guise-of-this-flesh –

Then in my dream, like a hawk,
I circled the garden:
No, it was the Earth, the grand, lacerated Earth;
On its whorled surface,
All the ages of humankind.

And a voice sang:
Here are flowers of deep suffering,
Swaying in the heart of God –

8

Because
      Each of us must seek
A finer life, a finer death.

Because
      In the garden, beside clematis,
Jousting with slippery shadows
Of birth-and-death-and-birth-and-death,
Sometimes I come back to
The pitiless floor of Hiroshima,
Knowing in the terror and magnitude
Of true comprehension
I meant to die there –
Back to the fierce moment
After the *pika*, the flash,
When suddenly I reclaimed
A small, clear
Flicker of self –
My flesh gone,
But my soul still singing,
Adamant to live:

The history of survival is written under my lids.

9

And if the husk of the world is ripped away,

We will not have altered the consciousness of one leaf –

Let this earth become a heaven:
From the point of light within the mind of God,
The Earth hurling its roughhouse wills and lusters,
The Earth accruing poison –
Planet of joy, planet of crucifixion,
Piñata destined to be smashed –
Ashes, ashes,
All the mirrors of heaven blackening, imagine:
No lack, no lack, but in our human minds –

Let the clematis become a prayer
As clouds and canon-flowers ready
Sweet unguents of pollen and rain,
As God bellows, and a wild cavalry of wind sweeps
Down from the houses of magic
Down from the houses of magic
Down from the houses of magic

for Elizabeth Eckford
Little Rock, Arkansas, 1957

Thick at the schoolgate are the ones
Rage has twisted
Into minotaurs, harpies
Relentlessly swift;
So you must walk past the pincers,
The swaying horns,
Sister, sister,
Straight through the gusts
Of fear and fury,
Straight through:
Where are you going?

I'm just going to school.

Here we go to meet
The hydra-headed day,
Here we go to meet
The maelstrom –

Can my voice be an angel-on-the-spot,
An amen corner?
Can my voice take you there,
Gallant girl with a notebook,
Up, up from the shadows of gallows trees
To the other shore:
A globe bathed in light,
A chalkboard blooming with equations –

I have never seen the likes of you,
Pioneer in dark glasses:
You won't show the mob your eyes,
But I know your gaze,
Steady-on-the-North-Star, burning –

With their jerry-rigged faith,
Their spear of the American flag,
How could they dare to believe
You're someone sacred?:
Nigger, burr-headed girl,
Where are you going?

I'm just going to school.

MARATHON

for Melvin Dixon
(1950–1992)

Sensuous and hilarious wit,
Nothing on this roiling, breakspirit earth
Could have readied you
For the doctors' stark edict:
There is a small window of time
To save your sight;
Choose your eyes,
And leave your lover's deathbed.

Choose, choose –
The word, keen as a scimitar:
Better to go blind, anointing
The chalice of his last breath?
Better to see, bereft
Of merciful closure? –

When the simoom of contagion –
Shared world, shared semen,
Shared needle, shared blood –
Is hushed at last,
Perhaps then I'll grasp
How you outpaced the minutes,
Hectoring wings,
How you raced home from surgery,
The lapis of the bay intact,
To his blessed persistence:

Love of my life, you can ebb now;
Being-without-end,
Pass your sight into me.

A COURTESY, A TRENCHANT GRACE

for Jim Giumentaro (1959–1992)
and for Terry Pitzner

Leaving you,
Knowing you would likely die
While I was away,
Made me recall
The photographer's tale,
How he ventured into a realm
Of monkey temples, rickshaws,
River-pilgrims, ghats,
The numinous city of Benares,
And discovered an urchin
Toppled in a clamorous street:
No one would touch him;
Not one among the merchants
Or mendicants.
He lifted the dust-checkered child,
Swabbed his hands, the russet
Planet of his face.
You understand,
The photographer was a man
Annealed by war,
Inured to suffering,
Yet at having to leave
The frayed child
Only rupees, a little food,
He felt his surgeon's soul unclappered.

But on his return
The following day, he found

The boy of the holy, moribund flesh,
The threadbare boy,
Upright;
The city of ash and fervent pilgrim's prayer
Seemed unstainable then,
The yogi's poise by the river
More radiant –

Jim, once we lay in the lee
Of the plague's unblooming
Gusts and battleground,
On a calm bed,
The gift which at the very last
Had to stand for
All my allegiance,
My living arms' goodwill:
I cradled you,
Mindful of your shingles,
Let you doze
For an unhaggard hour:
I was giving you my bed
To die in.
And in my grief and will
To absolution for what seemed
My gargantuan failure
To keep you alive,
It was as if I was fashioning
An inmost shrine,
An evensong to be stationed
Wherever on this earth
A courtesy, a trenchant grace
Is enacted
In the smallest gesture:
Soup spoon tucked

Under a lesioned lip,
Palm-and-lotion laving
A wand-lean leg;
Above the intravenous tube,
Or through a martyrdom of flies,
A true and level gaze
Is manna,
In laboring hospices,
In compassionless, dusty streets,

In the sacred city of Benares.

EVENING LASTING AS LONG AS LIFE

in memory of four friends

The force, the aureole
Of all you were,
Flooding the hospice,
On this evening lasting as long as life,
Streaming round the husk, the hollowed
Dovecote of your skin –
I am not disease only;
Hold me as you would hold
The body of Christ –
Everywhere echoes:
Words spoken in chatterhappy mischief,
Words spoken in dream-bitten anger and grief
That we will never grow old together:
Brushstrokes, hammerstrokes,
The uppermost passion to be –

It was a privilege
To wipe away your sweat and ordure,
To talk as never before,
To hush the ravings
The world ranged against you in fear,
The great aphrodisiac of the earth –
And always you were teaching me
The time-at-hand:
This moment, *this* pain,
This marvel, then the next –

Now you join the many
Men, women, and children,

"A generation of grass,"
Gone from us
In the plague time,
And the world of countinghouse glitter,
The knockabout, warring world,
Will never know rest
Or rightness,
Till the suffering of millions is quilted
Into a usable splendor –

On this evening lasting as long as life,
Let me dream your wick-thin arms
As estuaries – brisk, emboldened,
Outspanning the distance between
The life we imagined
And the life we had to learn:
The pageant-sure thrust of rivers
To the sea,
The urge and clement drift
Into the calmest lap,
The clear, the cradling light
Of death.

SUNG FROM A HOSPICE

Still craving a robust
Tenderness and justice,
I will go on living
With all I have seen:
Young men lusterless;
Against my blind cheek –
Blessed be the frangible
And dying,
The irreplaceable dead –
In my crestfallen arms:
With breath,
Then without it,
With flesh,
Then freed of it –

And the indurate man I heard
Condemn the stricken,
While my cousin was dying,
If he had walked these wards,
Armorless, open
To the imperiled,
Surely he would have gleaned
To sit in judgment
Is to sit in hell –

Lesions, elegies,
Disconnected phones –

Rain, nimble rain,
Be anodyne,

Anoint me
When I say outright:
In the plague time, my heart
Was tested,
My living soul
Struck like a tower bell,
Once, twice,
Four times in a single season.

THE WEIGHT OF BROTHERS

for Terry Pitzner
Afghan refugee camp, Peshawar, Pakistan

I. THE WEIGHT OF BROTHERS

At noon's ochre moment,
A man bows down
To pray beside a clinic wall,

A man who has lived a long time
On a violet hatful of mulberries –

The days are wreathed in a smoke
Of pell-mell horror and frailty –
Wheelbarrows always filling
With the injured, the unmoored.

Yet sometimes a boy will proffer
His supper scrap
To a whip-thin child,
Or a man will lift on his back
The maimed weight of another:

Brotherhood is portage,
Miraculous portage
Through the bombs, the guns' bluster.

Brotherhood is an eye
Unflinching, unable to stop
Cradling the defiled:

The match burst
At the shutter's gasp,
As the endangered man in the frame,
Face tattooed with debris,
Becomes family.

2. THE AFGHAN MEDICAL PHOTOGRAPHER

Peshawar, Pakistan

As a woman fills
The soft prison of her *chador*,
Raw, sinuous, will-o'-the-wisp –
So each strafed heart of half
The round earth's refugees
Brims with the toppled kingdom:

We are the Afghans;
From tents, mud huts,
Hunkered in dust, hot wind,
We dream back the land,
The ancient prize
Of many armies, ambitions,
Now the roaring of a million mines –

To survive a Goliath is grace,
A gleanable myrrh,
Cast by the still-alive,
Consigned to you
Who must bathe the injured
In a calm, invisible anodyne,
As you negotiate
The janitor's work of war,

As you kneel down
In a mosque of suffering:
A cinderblock room,
Redolent of green tea and Fanta,
Crowded with damaged men
Whose staunchest prayer
Is the bread and salt
Of root-deep brotherhood –

With blunt portraits,
You return from the Khyber,
Begging us to see:

The distance between privilege and carnage
Vanishes –
Extinguished by whatever tenderness
The stanching eye,
The soul in its entirety,
Can muster;

To see at all is grace:

This child offers the camera
His blighted gaze.
This man peers through a mask of fire;

It has come to this:
Hen feathers, rubble, shards of broken dolls,
Rubbish from the pockets
Of a Russian soldier's corpse,
Culled from the dust
Of his gutted shelter;
A tourniquet of turban cloth:
His blood and shock

Carried on a ragged mule
Through the winter-toothed mountains,
Over the poisoned ground,
Under hoary stars, grenades
Strapped to kites,
Over the border,
A cusp of iced trees,
To the camp –

For years his people have lived,
Weaving the pterodactyl arcs
Of helicopters,
The glare of baleful tanks,
Into garish and defiant rugs –

And although this warrior-from-a-hailstorm's
Hand is ruined,
He has placed behind his shrapneled ear
Rich petals:

Here on the lens, one human flourish,
Countering the wounding,
The carrion and conflagration:

Rose of the singed and hungry world,
Ever-cooling rose.

3. HOMAGE

Beside the pleasurable blue, the bay view,
He has stoically enshrined,
On a desk rich with eucalyptus,
Adjacent to the bed,

The photograph of an injured
Mujahideen,
Beside the gull's sweep,
The dory in the wave –

A man whose gaze is interrupted
By a bloodied chrysanthemum
Seared to his cheek, a bloom
He must go on bearing and bearing
Through the roughhouse world –

I ask the photographer, how can he rest
With the desecrated man
So close?

And he answers
That now he perceives, above all,
The undiminished eye;
Look at it, he dares.

And yes, there is something there, something
Even truer than the wound:
Vibrance, intelligence reclaimed
From dust, from agony.

And now I understand
This is not penitence but homage.

THE TOSS

I see a knife-grinder
On his dusty, stationary bicycle,
A black Star of David
Sprayed over a door,
As you urge me
Into the rationed light,
The crumbling pearl-grey
Of the ghetto.
All at once, the Roman spring,
With its galaxy of columns
And daisies,
Becomes the autumn of families
Plummeting from windows,
The desecrated autumn
Your mother tossed you,
Small bundle,
To a passerby.
Like this, you demonstrate
With a parcel.

But what can't be mimed
Is the look they shared,
The look that let you live,
Her toss that had to be
Quick, quick,
Before the cat-pounce Nazis came –
Out the shutters,
Into the samaritan's determined arms:
Something unerring
Passing through the air
Of an iron universe –

As the knife-grinder pedals and pedals,
You whisper: *I know nothing*
Of what became of her.

Perhaps she soothed a boy
Born in the *Lager*,
Listless, mute,
Whose Lilliputian arm
Bore the tattoo of Auschwitz.
She would have coaxed him
To lift his intransigent eyes,
Knowing you might also be
Somewhere among the living.

And against the jackboot, the demolition,
For as long as she was able, she

Poem for the Artists of the Holocaust

The bone-white wind of this century
A prayer-shawl of human ash.
And still the hand lifts
The intrepid pencil,
The chip of charcoal,
Against the plunder, the ordure, the roaring.

And still the soul craves to make bridgeable
The space between the careworn
And the dead,
Craves never to quit the embattled earth
Unrecorded,
The unstainable soul:

This is the charnel house art,
The epistle,
Cached in the sleep-safe tin,
Inviolable, brought to air:

Dear Finder,

In Terezin,
By the meager bread-carts,
In Auschwitz,
Beside the rooms of shaved hair –
Tell someone I was here.

THE RETURN OF THE LIVING WITNESS

for Eric Kahn
Terezin, Czechoslovakia

A child's fist-hard vow never to forget
The taste of grass,
Never to laugh again,
Becomes, at last, a summons:

Now the child is a pewter-haired man
Who parts,
With a cane of dogged memory,
Piercing as a cantor's topmost note,
The innocuous stillness, the chill air
Of Terezin:

Rancorless, with a sense of justice,
He walks the garden, the avenues
Once forbidden to the Jews –

The black potatoes,
The curl of flesh
Ensnared on the thorny wire,
Gone, and not gone:

Gingerly, the living witness fords
Two realms,
One of silence,
One of asp-cold yellow stars.

He finds, in time, the dour barracks;
It was in this drafty room

That he began, in German,
The poem that would take him
Forty years and another language
To finish:

Dunkel Gestalten, gebückt und bedrückt
Mit diesen ist die Strasse bestückt.

The street is filled with gnarled apparitions,
Hollow ghosts…

THESE ARE NOT BRUSHSTROKES

in homage to Picasso's Guernica,
seen in Madrid

The planes flew low over the house;
Luna the maid quailed,
Crossed herself to the infinite power,
And fainted

The bombs shattered Time;
Now the stars are smothered,
Unreachable

In the gutted precincts,
Not *Good morning*,
But *How many of your family*
Are still alive?

O my daughter, your wedding's on Sunday;
I wonder if the groom will take you
Without legs

The woman gaped at her house –
Capsized, outlandish,
Open to the wind:
"But señor, I have no politics…"

And then he turned and saw
A young girl thrashing beyond
A barricade of dead horses

Under the wreckage they found me,

Like Cleopatra,
Curled into a rug

Because victory's equivalent to
Slandered corpses,
Implacable kings,
Blood in the scepter's shadow

Shh! What's that sound?

As the condemned priest raised his hand
To bless me,
One of my bullets
Pierced the center of his palm

The soldier in my garden
Was from the wrong side.
His jaw was broken.
He was bleeding.
Still I believed,
With a child's pure terror,
He could kill me.
But he pressed into my hand
A perfect berry

SEARCH

*for Lorca
in Granada*

There was the gentle hearsay of the wind in the corn,
Two men bending, noon-drenched, in the orchard:
After an hour of combing, desperate
To find some trace, to beg you back,
I found your home, obscured
By a shield of cypress.
No marker. Only dust
And vigilant dogs –

But you predicted this,
Your wine-maculate moment:

*When pure forms collapsed
Beneath daisies' cries, I realized
They had murdered me.
They ransacked cafés, cemeteries, churches,
They opened wine-casks…
Yet they never found me:*

No, prophet, poet of mercury,
Your body was never found.

❖

I was walking in the Albaicín,
Each breath, each step, gravid with jasmine;
The umber hills had darkened,
As well as the cool, galactic

40

Voluble rooms of the Alhambra,
When a gypsy appeared,
Wheedling a brief train of donkeys
Bearing a cargo of gaudy rugs;
As I watched them negotiate
A daunting, skeletal street,
I heard him singing:

If my heart had windowpanes…
If I could mount the wind
As it sweeps
Through the chilly grove,
Where the green moon loiters…

I listened
Till the well-deep, plentiful singing luffed

And lingered, lingered, lingered.

THE REQUEST

for Konstantine Azadovsky
Leningrad, 1986

Then you marked the innocuous place, the dark
Bookshelf where the drug was planted,
The drug they used to frame you –
In the grip of that nearly white night,
That brief but vital darkness,
You struggled to describe
A thousand and one arctic nights,
And I wanted to bolt,
My mind drumming:
Don't take me there;
Don't make me have to imagine…

When I think of how
They beat you with the steel
Of your prison door
Till you were barely conscious
For your own trial,
How each day they brick-and-mortar to make you
An *unperson*,
I bow to you,
In your once-ransacked study –
Orphan-tough temple
With pews of human speech –
Always under surveillance,
With its treasured books,
Its miniature of Pushkin
Above the desk –

I came to you by chance,
From a rousing party
Of poets, puppeteers,
Diplomats and Russian rock stars,
And your shrike-stern tale
Was like a dark scrim laid across
The drinks and soothing laughter –

There was no time to ask
What last hoarded match, what holy memory
Sustained you,
Beside the filthy plank bed, in the prison yard
Tamped with ice –

Forgive me if I need to dream
In a world where poets
Scratch verses into bars of soap,
And brave scholars are beaten,
Disavowed;
If I need to dream you
Beyond undoing,
And can hardly imagine
The dread, the daily erosion:

What can I do for you?

Don't forget me.

To the cypress again and again

in memory of Salvador Espriu
(1913–1985)

When Franco's regime came to power, the
Catalan language was banned from public use,
and Salvador Espriu, a literary prodigy, sud-
denly found himself unable to publish.

Sinera (Arenys de Mar, Spain)

I woke to ash in my mouth:
Don't bark! Speak the language of the Empire!

Everywhere silence, dispiriting silence.
Old men fined on the streets;
Children whipped
For a single word:

It was like the dream of Joseph in Egypt,
The dream in the dungeon, the dank well,
Or the plangent cry of Job,
The fortunate man who wakes in hell,
Tested by a fire from heaven –

❖

Beside the cypress, for a while I could believe
God was not dead –
Under the first avid stars;
He had spared my country:

In light and shadow, in merciful beauty,
My village arrayed,
And beneath the yoke of solitude,
A distant majesty of dolphins –

❖

In those ardent days of the Republic,
Years of shared bread,
My language filled me
Like heady wine,
Laced with a sweetness of figs,
Tang of pine nuts – my country
An almond tree in bloom,
The Mediterranean my garden –
Blue, voluminous –

But then came armies of the dead –

Sometimes I'd sit before the blank, impoverished page,
Till the rising sun reclaimed
Hills of vines and fennel,
And from wide fields would come
Voices of peasants,
Mingling with voices of my dead,
The sound of hoes striking my heart –

Always I was seeking
Something more than Cervantes.
More than the brutal pantomime of war.
More than the brunt of the black boot.
More than sin or the minotaur.
More, more than the fear of death –

An alphabet of cypress and sea-light.

❖

Cassells,
The name could be Mallorcan –

How old are you?:

Twenty-seven,
And you've never read *Don Quixote*!

❖

To the cypress, to the scintillant blue
Dress of the Mediterranean
Swishing off to the Balearics,
Year after year, you climbed,
To the cemetery with its hush of marble –
Your language like sweetly-guarded seeds
In your breastpocket:

At any moment
You could have tossed them to the wind –

I reached your village:
How the cemetery crowns Sinera!
The wind ushered me to
Your corridor of cypress:
Wondrous trees that listen
And answer back.
So I asked for the hard word you cherished
Between ancient boundaries
Of vineyards and sea.

Like gods, in green unison, the cypress let go
In lucent whisper:

Liberty.

❖

Bring me all the adjectives of the rock –
Adamant, tenacious, obstinate, unwavering –
For Salvador Espriu is dead –

You slipped away from me
So quickly, Espriu,
Yet blessed me
With the subtlest gift:

The wealth and mystery of our single meeting –

❖

It was beyond the Pyrenees, in Perpignan,
That I saw it for the first time:
Families streaming from their tables to begin
The *sardana*, your native dance,
Banned for many years,
A deft, living circle
Mirroring sunrise –
The light, a dawn of hands
Linked in deep Mediterranean laughter.

❖

Cyrus, when Franco died, the champagne vanished
From all the hoary shelves of Sinera.

I held a glass to my lips –
The taste was keen, unimaginably kind –
And I called to my missing, my dead, to return
From the manacled kingdoms of exile.
Then I climbed to my battlement of lush trees.

NIGHT AND MIST

For Claribel Alegría and Carolyn Forché

I

And then the voice of authority:
      Your people were never slaughtered,
      Never lost.
      Your massacres were only dreams –

Nacht und Nebel, the Nazis called
Their handiwork, their human erasure:

Torturers, tyrants, counterfeits and kings,
They would shroud cities
      In bleach and denial,
      Blood and euphemism,
      Night and mist.

2

Did you know her?
The woman shunted into the blindfold,
Into brutal hands,
Cries and gashes of silence,
Whispers-become-daily-bread.
The woman who gave birth
In that place stripped of the feminine.

The woman whose child was stolen,
Whose child now sits

49

At the torturer's table,
Calling him *father, father*...
The woman who wrote with tears, fingernails, coal.
The woman who washed away
The writing on the walls:
Mene, mene, tekel, upharsin –

Did you know her?
They say she was "disappeared."

The woman who laughed
And drank *maté* in the morning.
The woman who read the Gospel to the poor.
The woman with the placard in the Plaza de Mayo,
Defiant against generals.

The woman who was numinous, demeaned.
The woman whose limbs were beaten,
Whose heart was sacked,
Whose dissident beauty
Was dumped in the sea.
The woman who survives,
If only in memory:

The woman who can never be erased.

3

The drawn shutters of the feudal mansion.
Bougainvillea. Adobe walls.
The deception of a normal life –

A downcast stillness, then
Dust plumes at the rim of the field,
As a death squad races
Toward its panting target:
Hunted figure trapped
In the havoc of the here-and-now –

And one of them will batter,
And one will sting,
And one will slash,
Each man spattered, in turn,
Because none must remain sinless –

Is there no way out of the heart
Beating *let me live, let me live?*

No way out of these frenzied hands,
With their fierce purchases of blood?

4

If mere death no longer instills
Fear in the population,
Line roads, litter fields
With bodies.
Give the trees garlands
Of hair, human skin.
Make Spanish another language
For mourning.

5

All night listening to Marcelino's tale:
How he burrowed in an attic,
While a death squad butchered his brother;
He was heart-gutted,
Unable to flee the sounds...

Marcelino in prison,
Falling and falling on the thin ice
Of electric shock;
In solitary:
When an ant or a fly strayed
Into his shipwreck of a cell,
It became a jubilee.

6

Today I read
The testimony of Jacobo Timerman:
How he stood in a helldark cell
In Buenos Aires, dressed in his own excrement,
Playing hide-and-seek – the guards had left
The judas-hole ajar –
With the poignant, luminous eyes
Of his comrade-in-torture.
He was trying to make me a gift
Of that gaze,
But how could he
Give it away,
Since it was priceless, since it was

Pure communion,
Which has no currency
In this misted world.

A SHADRACH CHORUS

for Susan Griffin
and for Charlotte Solomon
(1917–1943)

1

Through avenues of immeasurable burning,
Fire beyond belief,
Fire unabated,
In beleaguered
Dresden-become-a-pyre,
She found herself allied
With a lion licked by flames,
Soot-streaked, tawny monarch,
Exiled from a cindered zoo –
The two, war-cornered king
And consort,
Spurred to the salve-cool
River for refuge –
Maunderers unaware
This fist-fast vehemence,
This crucible is called
A firestorm:
This pleading for an allaying
Mother of water.

2

Because he heard pleading
From the battlefield's red vandalism

For two confounding days,
An unreachable, bell-clear cry.

Because 1917, a carnage
Gravid with gas-masks,
Droves of greatcoats,
Crushed whole fields and meadows
Of his memory.

Because he caught
In the moribund calls
Of unraveling soldiers
High notes deemed
Impossible for men to make:
Wracked warriors with the tree-tall
Crests of coloraturas.

This is how the stretcher-bearer became
A maestro of voice.

3

He is here again,
Her maestro and lover,
Amid the mud-drenched days,
The babel of the barracks,
Where she isn't even a name,
Where she isn't even
Charlotte Solomon
Of the bold self-portraits,
But digits in skin.

He is here,
Invisible in Auschwitz,
Saying *Even if your voice cracks...*
Coaxing *Go ahead, Charlotte,*
Explore the cracks,
And inside her demeaned,
Supernumerary flesh,
She is marshaling
Her cabaret frankness,
Her trenchant colors,
To combat a fearsome web
Of family suicides,
And she is singing as she daubs
The elating brush,
Alive to the fissures,
Unabashed.

4

And when his plague-weary love
Tried to hasten closure
With a clothesline noose,
Against the coma's palisades,
Emilio began to sing,
With all his being,
Once-unknowable notes,

And with his hospice *a cappella*,
Rolled the stone away –

Never knowing he was one
With the shell-shocked maestro,

The painter behind thorny wire,
Singing a bit
As she relinquished her sketch
For a thimbleful of thread;

One with the Shadrach girl
On the riverbank,
Whose sound arcs
Above spellbinding, obliterating flames:
A girl with the cataract grief
Of a lion;
A lion with the treble wail
Of a trembling girl –

Even if your voice cracks,
Speaker, fallible singer,
In a century of immeasurable burning,
Tell me something true.

LIFE INDESTRUCTIBLE

for Etty Hillesum
(1914–1943)

1

It might have been a sibyl's voice,
Clear and winnowing:

We should be willing to act as a balm for all wounds.

All winter I've slept and labored
With those words.
Etty, you've haunted me –
I can't stop hearing your voice,
The last line of your diary,
Unshakable:

We should be willing to act as a balm for all wounds
We should be willing to act as a balm
We should be willing to act
We should be willing...

2

Your voice, Etty Hillesum,
A young Dutch Jew
Avid to weave a self
Whose ardent story
Refuses to end
In bleakness,

The final seep of ash,
Refuses to end
With your cloaked, anonymous death –

3

Like a wave long embedded in your body –
Your urge to kneel,
Bear witness –

Dear "thinking heart of the barracks,"
When you started your diary
One loutish spring, in an occupied city,
You chose to listen to your soul:

Very well then, this new certainty
That what they are after
Is our total destruction.
I accept it. I know it now
And I will not burden others
With my fears.
I will not be bitter
If others fail to grasp
What is happening…
I work and continue to live
With the same conviction –

4

There was a man you came to love,
A priest of Jung,
Cherished by many women

For his warlock's gift:
Unraveling the map of the hand –
That second face, you called it.

Matchless union:
All at once you're negotiating a field
Of fierce clarity – lavender, lavender,
An ardor of lavender –

And you carried this strange sentience
Into a lovers' city
Of flower stalls, little bridges,
Become a city slowly siphoned of Jews...

Yet you stuck to your lucent journey,
As lovers might:
Reading the *Song of Solomon*
After rations,
Taking blackout paper from the window
To watch the stars –

You vowed to follow him
Even to flinty camps,
Sharing his fate –
Dear spoiled man,
Who died in his own bed
On the glowering day
The Nazis set for his capture –

5

You volunteered for Westerbork,
Way station to Poland:

No, not enough to love God from a garret,
When everywhere your people are reviled.
My people – yes, the words have a weight;
You feel them,
A well-worn treasured key
Cached between your breasts,
And so you go to your tribe,
Simply.

6

Behind barbed wire,
The one, unchanging task:
To value each
Who crosses your path –

Like the haggard, hunchbacked woman
In her green silk kimono,
Who came to you in Westerbork,
Moving with weird grace
From bed to bed,
Doing small services for the damned:

Surely God will understand my doubts
In a world like this...

7

Down on my knees, I begin to understand,
Dear girl who was learning to kneel –
With my forehead pressed
To the cool and charitable ground:

Yes, there are places the mind can't go,
Suffused as it is
With an inner debris,
Where only the soul can enter,
As the heart is crushed beneath the wheels
Of that juggernaut we call
Past and future:
The gutless Never Now,
The Never Here –

So you have to kneel
In the instant
When hush and humility are all;
You have to kneel
With a lilylike trust,

As you await the flutter of God…

8

Time and again, the trek to Poland,
The train's prey-cry,
Titanic, metallic –
Sometimes a rag or beloved hand
Waving from obstinate gaps
In box cars –

In brilliant, arduous light,
Now freight trains fill
With plundered heiresses, and bawling infants,
The old glazier, barely clothed,
Clutching a frayed, last-minute blanket –

The gruff boy who failed to escape,
And catapulted forty souls
Into the wide seine
Of corporal punishment,
The ex-soubrette adding hairdye
To her suitcase,
The fettered gypsies, and the light-shy nuns,
The old women asking:
Will there be medical assistance in Poland?

9

At the threshold of banishment
There is so little to clasp,
Or carry.
Very well then,
You'll clear room in the rucksack
For Rilke, a Russian grammar,
A small, hardy Bible;
Opening the pages at random, you find:
The Lord is my high tower...

Is there room for Tolstoy on the train to Auschwitz?

You've made room.

❖

And now you toss from the train
An incandescent postcard:

We have left the camp singing –

Today I went out into the sun,
With your injunction to *feel*,
Refuse every soporific,
To step into both
The bitter and the blossoming:

Beyond crocuses,
Always judges-and-juries,
The shadows of bully pulpits,
Of gallows trees –

And if I can hear long-voweled clues
Of blackbirds,
Red-wing clarions of spring,
Then I must hear
My neighbors groaning –

Etty, you journeyed to the core
Of havoc:

And if I should not survive,
How I die
Will show me who I really am:

Tell me what you found.
Tell me what it means
When a young man answers:
My AIDS – that's when the blessings began,
That's when I turned
To face my true self –

Today when I boarded a train,
I stood before a woman so deformed,
I felt the whole enormous weight –
Common fear, disgust, apathy, decorum –
The whole Valhalla of cruel culture
Against my cheek,
So that it took sheer strength
Not to turn away,
Sheer strength to let my eye veer
Into a place, a holiness
That was utterly hers –
Sheer strength for her to bare herself
To the workaday world –
Extraordinary woman,
Bloated mask,
Won-back heart
In her plain but confident business suit.

And it was your voice I imagined then:

If they speak of fate,
Terrific suffering,
Tell them:
We were never in anyone's "clutches";
Always, always,
We were in the arms of God.

FLEUR

No, it is not suffering that engenders it;
              it is beyond suffering,
The Flower –
              though it rests beside
the tears, the million barricades,
              fusillade upon fusillade…
it rests,
              soft as a fontanel.

❖

Fifty-four whales beach on the shore,
              vials of blood, and syringes,
so that we might perceive The Flower,
              cry out for it.

❖

With sternness and delicacy,
              Georgia O'Keeffe,
that clear-eyed woman,
              leaned into its sacred warmth,
with her paints,
              her probity.

❖

Yes, its stem is like
              the jammed, astonishing column of crutches
the healed leave behind,
              a column of miracles

in a snowlit, hallowed shrine.

❖

      Stopping on the road to Tula,
to Tolstoy's estate,
      I found a flower
like one from my childhood,
      a great seraphic bloom.
But there were missiles between it
      and its Western twin,
missiles!, missiles!,
      and a killing mystique.

❖

Not long after Chernobyl's gasp,
      I looked from a window
in Dostoyevsky's house,
      and watched a man pass a sinister wand
over the vegetables for market,
      over the flowers.

❖

How much can the petals withstand,
      while we hasten the leavings,
the radioactive waste?

❖

      It cannot last,
this juggernaut, this whirlwind futility:
      surely joy will outdistance

the century's mass graves,
  the earth's furious junkyards;
surely joy will outdistance us.

  ❖

  A woman strokes the numerals
seared forever into her skin,
  and with deadsure fingers examines
stark photographs from the war:
  this happened to me,
and this –
  and still I survived…
Yes, there were lupines in the camp,
  and our joy in them was real,
as real as our misery.
  We would find some little corner of the barracks
to put them on display;
  we would pick and scoop them into our arms,
after a day of forced labor.

  ❖

  Oh once, during the war,
there was a boy,
  bewildered, deaf from birth,
unable to comprehend
  the men in dark uniforms barking
Jew, Jew,
  get down on your knees! –
so that his father had to coax him
  to touch the paving with his mouth,
to take part in the wretched street cleaning.

And after wetting a stone
with a sullen tongue,
            the boy found his work
had made it shine.

            Then ridicule, and bullying hatred,
then indignity gave way
            to something rapt – gave way
to sheer accomplishment.

            Undaunted, he found a tiny flower-shape
set deep into the stone,
            let its brief, invisible pollen brush him.

And for that one instant, let me believe,
            the universe was moved;
all the gall of the day
            was changed to wine:

ma fleur, ma fleur...

Oh what would you give to find that flower?

CODA

In the years of grave listening,
The Passion was with me,
A Christ of quicklime,
Of groaning tumbrels –
I lived in a garden – lush, inordinate,
Yet more and more besieged
By cries and clashing:
Turk-cap lilies, missiles!, missiles!, and men
Shouting a thousand military chants
Against the earth –

From my green seat of privilege,
I heard voices
Of torture, testimony,
Insistent voices:
Look, Golgotha has widened
Into the world –

And whenever I quailed,
Pasqueflowers, cypress,
Irises of slender poise
Imbued me with their strength,
Elms I once imagined
As Gethsemane's anchored olives:

All these crosses, legacies,
Spirits leading me in crescendo
To a place where at last
I could acknowledge
My deepest fears –
Crucifixion, humiliation, hunger –

A place where in time
I could recognize
A faith, a perseverance
Almost unseen, barely recorded,
Beyond the wrack's gleam,
The blue theater
Where humanity is flayed:

The secret history of the earth –

Christ-of-clear-panoramas,
In my Holy Week dream
Of famine,
I was a woman rooted
To a flinty Ukrainian field –
Cracked peasant boots, frayed
Babushka of peonies –
My arms burdened
With swart, filthy potatoes,
My last ration.
And I was whimpering,
For they had come for it,
Cursing, indigent soldiers,
With their hard jewelry of guns –
There were shouts, a sibilance, and then I saw
They had taken her from me too,
My little girl,
With something sharp –
As I reached, then clung to her
In that abject field –

❖